JP
MCLE

A Little Ark Book
First published 1997
by Allen & Unwin Pty Ltd
9 Atchison Street
St Leonards, NSW 2065
Australia
Phone: (61 2) 9901 4088
Fax: (61 2) 9906 2218
E-mail: frontdesk@allen-unwin.com.au
URL: http://www.allen-unwin.com.au

National Library of Australia
Cataloguing-in-Publication entry:

McLean, Janet, 1946– .
    Josh.

    ISBN 1 86448 362 8 (hb)
    ISBN 1 86448 490 X (pb)

    I. McLean, Andrew, 1946– . II. Title.

A823.3
1. Dogs-Fiction

Designed and typeset by Beth McKinlay
Produced in Australia by The Australian Book Connection.

1 0 9 8 7 6 5 4 3 2

JOSH

Written by Janet McLean
Illustrated by Andrew McLean

A LITTLE ARK BOOK

ALLEN & UNWIN

This is Josh. He's my friend.

He wakes me up in the morning,

and then we make the bed.

He helps me get dressed,

and I give him breakfast.

Josh follows me everywhere.

Aaaagh!

But sometimes he likes to go first.

Jump Josh

I'm teaching Josh some tricks.

We like playing games together.

My favourite is
'What's the time, Mr Wolf?'

Josh likes 'Bring in the washing'

and 'Find the bone'.

At night we have a bath,

and play 'Hide and Seek'.

Josh always finds me.

Then we read a bedtime story.
Goodnight, Josh.